Why Do We Celebrate INDEPENDENCE DAY?

Jonathan Potter

PowerKiDS press.

New York

Published in 2019 by The Rosen Publishing Group, Inc.
29 East 21st Street, New York, NY 10010

First Edition

Editor: Brianna Battista
Book Design: Reann Nye

Photo Credits: Cover Ivan Marc/Shutterstock.com; p. 5 Monkey Business Images/Shutterstock.com; p. 6 Robert Pernell/Shutterstock.com; p. 9 JohnKwan/Shutterstock.com; p. 10 Valeriya Zankovych/Shutterstock.com; p. 13 Jose Luis Pelaez Inc/Blend Images/Getty Images; pp. 14, 24 wavebreakmedia/Shutterstock.com; pp. 17, 24 Blend Images- KidStock/ Brand X Pictures/Getty Images; p. 18 VisionsofAmerica/Joe Sohm/DigitalVision/Getty Images; p. 21 Ariel Skelley/DigitalVistion/Getty Images; pp. 22, 24 (fireworks) nd3000/Shutterstock.com.

Cataloging-in-Publication Data

Names: Potter, Jonathan.
Title: Why do we celebrate Independence Day? / Jonathan Potter.
Description: New York : PowerKids Press, 2019. | Series: Celebrating U.S. holidays | Includes index.
Identifiers: LCCN ISBN 9781508166450 (pbk.) | ISBN 9781508166436 (library bound) | ISBN 9781508166467 (6 pack)
Subjects: LCSH: Fourth of July–Juvenile literature. | Fourth of July celebrations–Juvenile literature.
Classification: LCC E286.P68 2019 | DDC 394.2634 –dc23

Manufactured in the United States of America

CPSIA Compliance Information: Batch #CS18PK: For Further Information contact Rosen Publishing, New York, New York at 1-800-237-9932

CONTENTS

Independence Day is on July 4.
It's America's birthday!

Independence Day celebrates the 13 American colonies becoming the United States.

Thomas Jefferson wrote the Declaration of Independence in 1776. It became official on July 4.

Many Americans celebrate Independence Day. It's also called the Fourth of July.

The Fourth of July is a summer holiday. People celebrate outside together.

Families and friends get together for picnics. They cook food on the **grill**.

There are **parades** on Independence Day. People carry American flags.

17

18

The national parade is in Washington, D.C. The president lives in Washington, D.C.

The American flag is red, white, and blue. People wear these colors to celebrate.

People watch **fireworks** at night. Fireworks light up the sky!

23

Words to Know

fireworks

grill

parade

Index

Websites

Due to the changing nature of Internet links, PowerKids Press has developed an online list of websites related to the subject of this book. This site is updated regularly. Please use this link to access the list: www.powerkidslinks.com/ushol/indep